BRIAN JACQUES

The Great Redwall Feast

illustrated by
Christopher Denise

SCHOLASTIC INC.
New York Toronto London Auckland Sydney

To Jade Pascal Jacques,
from her grandfather
—*B.J.*

For my parents
—*C.D.*

Patricia Lee Gauch, Editor.
Type design by Patrick Collins. The text is set in Perpetua Bold.

ISBN 0-590-64750-4

12 11 10 9 8 7 6 5 4 3 2 1   8 9/9 0 1 2 3/0

Printed in the U.S.A.   14

First Scholastic printing, September 1998

I'll tell you a story,
you'll see it unfold.
I can still recall it, though I'm old.
'Tis an ancient tale,
related in rhyme,
which happened, once upon a time.

5

Once on a summer's day
in the golden long-ago
at the Abbey of Redwall (which some of you may know),
lots of woodland creatures
and all the Abbeymice
were planning in secret, a marvelous feast
for their abbot. Now wasn't that nice!

They bustled and hustled,
they hurried and scurried,
flittered and skittered and skipped.
From woodland to larder,
from orchard to cellar,
provisions were furtively shipped.

Trundling, bundling,
harrying, carrying,
tugging and lugging in force,
whilst good Father Abbot
sat taking his nap.
(He didn't know of the feast, of course!)

Giggling, chuckling,
whispering low,
smuggling, huddling creatures would go
with stifled laughter
and twinkling eyes.
Now wasn't their abbot in for a surprise!

Come...follow your nose
down into the kitchen.
There's fat Friar Hugo, in charge of it all.
Boiling, bubbling,
busily simmering;
herbs and dried roots hang thick from each wall.

"Chop up the chestnuts,
add some more apples,
pass me those damsons, and that meadowcream!"
His high squeaky voice
rises up to the rafters
'mid lovely aromas, and wispy white steam.

Breads and cheeses,
nuts and salads,
soups and pastries, pies and flans,
tarts and trifles,
cakes and puddings,
ovens, caldrons, pots and pans.

Stews and sauces,
jams and junkets,
candied fruits and honey sweets.
Baking, basting,
cooking, cooling,
festive fare and banquet treats.

Hark, stop and be still!
Is the old abbot waking?
His paws atwitching, he snuffles a mite.
Whispers Constance the badger,
good mother of Redwall,
"We should have done all this preparing last night!"

Matthias the Warrior
peeps at the sleeper.
"Oh dear, if he wakens, then what shall we do?"
Cornflower, his wife,
thinks up a solution.
"Take him for a stroll in the woodland with you.

"I know Father Abbot
is so fond of walking.
Why, earlier this morn, ere he sat down to rest,
I heard him and Foremole,
they were both talking
of going to Mossflower Wood . . . on a quest."

Without any warning
the abbot stands upright.
Yawning and blinking, he gives a great smile.
With a nod to the trio
he bids them good morning,
saying, "I've not been out on a stroll for a while,

"and listen, friends,
  this may sound odd,
  I quest for a *Bobbatan Weary Nod*.
  If you'll agree
  to accompany me,
  we'll see what we shall see!"

  A *Bobbatan Weary Nod?*

All through the great Abbey
stand helpers awatching,
murmuring low, like breeze in long grass.
"Our abbot must go.
Hush, don't let him know,
not a peep or a sound, stand aside, let him pass!"

Away 'cross the grounds
in sundewed morn
go Constance, Matthias, the abbot too,
when up pops Foremole
from out of the lawn.
"Gudd mornen, zurr Abbot, oi'm cummen wi' you!"

A squirrel sentry
named Noisy Sam
(after the friends have gone),
from high on the wall
roars out to all,
"All clear, back to work, everyone!"

Pushing and pulling,
heaving and weaving,
ducking and dodging, busying 'round.
Mixing and molding,
kneading and pawing,
lifting, shifting, as tasks are found.

Hear good Ambrose Spike,
a stout cellar master,
to his hedgehogs working like peas in a pod:
"Stir those quills,
we'll have to toil faster.
Hmph! Quest for a Bobbatan Weary Nod!

"It must be his age,
  seasons bless the old fellow.
  He'll forget that he's abbot before very long!
  His paws are adither,
  his mind has gone mellow.
  To work, hogs, let's strike up our song!"

"Whoooooooooooooaaaah!
  Cask an' barrel,
  keg an' firkin,
  autumn cider laid in stock.
  Rosehip syrup,
  strawb'rry cordial,
  dandelion an' old burdock.

*"*Bang! Bang! *the coopers hammer,*
  Glug! Glug! *the flagon fills.*
  Fruit juice of every manner
  banishes all ills."

Whilst out in the kitchen
there's much consternation.
Oh, hear a poor molemother's gruff, anguished cry.
"Waow! Moi liddle Bungo,
he'm only a h'infant,
gone an' falled into yon big tater pie!"

All 'round the huge basin
the moles and Friar Hugo,
with long wooden paddles they probe and they seek,
as Bungo's young sister
pipes up to their mother,
"Ee'll 'ave eaten 'is way outer thurr boi nex' week!"

Midst turnip and gravy,
potato and beetroot,
they scour and poke to the poor molemum's cries.
"Waow! Cain't yew find nothin',
a paw or a molesuit?
Be they bits o' beetroot, or are they 'is eyes?"

When up strolls young Bungo,
the sight of the season,
from tailtip to ears clad in damson and cream.
"Yurr Muther, 'tis Bungo.
Oi falled in a *plum* pie.
'Twere so delishuss oi diddent dare scream!"

Yonder's the veteran,
Basil "Stag" Hare.
He and Cornflower pick blossoms with care—
harebell and honeydew,
sweet columbine—
to grace the tables at banquet time.

Daisy and marigold,
primrose and lily . . .
they ramble on, quite willy-nilly.
Basil's convinced
of the abbot's folly.
"To me," he says, "a banquet sounds jolly,

"but a *Bobbatan Quest*
for a *Weary Nod*?
What d'you think? Sounds rather odd!
Let's hope our abbot
gets back all right,
or he'll miss his very own feast tonight!"

Fragrant blushing scarlet,
lilac and pale gold,
laden down with flowers, all their paws can hold.
Past the tranquil orchard,
'round the gable wall,
a scented rainbow drifts into the Abbey's hall.

Through stained glass windows,
high in Great Hall,
sunlight lances dustily down,
painting islands
of harlequin hues
on floorstones, timeworn, brown.

Three banquet tables
are set open-squared
in snow-white linen arrayed.
Such elegant grace,
no spoon out of place,
each plate, correctly laid.

Enjoying the shade
of a tapestried wall
in the timeless, silent, ancient hall,
they set down burdens,
all labors cease
to savor a moment of peace.

Then Basil's long ears
shoot up like twin spears.
"D'ye hear that? Somethin's crunchin'!"
Beneath the flowers
strewn on the floor,
there comes a sound of munching.

Carefully, cautiously,
Cornflower stoops,
stirs the blossoms, and peeps beneath.
There lies Bungo
bolting the blooms,
a marigold clenched in his teeth.

He plucks it out
and tugs his snout
politely, with roguish charm.
"This yurr salad
you uns picked
tastes vurry noice, thankee marm!"

Green gold of leaf and sun,
sweet birdsong on the air,
summertime in Mossflower, enchanting.
Staff in paw, the abbot strides
right well for one so old.
In his wake three comrades come apanting.

The stumbling, bumbling trio
share but a single thought:
Bobbatan Quest, Weary Nod, a journey all for naught?
"Listen to that nightingale,
ah, what a joyous song!"
A chuckling abbot chides them. "Keep up now, come along!"

Upon a fallen beechlog,
the followers sit awhile.
"Bet you're tired and hungry," says the abbot with a smile.
"Nothing like a woodland stroll
to whet one's appetite.
You'll enjoy supper all the more, when we return tonight."

Oaks in quiet noontide,
serene as guardians stand
o'er four Abbeydwellers in their forestland.
High above the foliage,
borne upon the breeze,
Redwall bells ring from afar out across the trees!

Disaster! Calamity!
Down in the cellars
a barrel of dandelion fizz has just burst!
With Noisy Sam roaring,
"All paws to the rescue!"
they stampede the staircase to get down there first.

Squirting and spurting,
spraying and sputtering,
a great oaken barrel like some savage beast
gushes fizz high and wide,
as it spins a mad circle.
"Misfortune!" wails Ambrose. "The day of the feast!"

Slipping and skidding,
dodging the barrel,
youngsters chase 'round with mouths open wide.
No sense in wasting,
it's so lovely tasting,
and dandelion fizz always tickles inside!

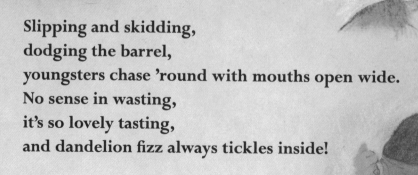

Make way, stand aside
for the Skipper of Otters!
He's weathered all storms of river and stream.
With a bung and a mallet,
the lithe, brawny creature
bounds upward to hang by his tail from a beam.

When the barrel speeds by,
Skipper's sharp roving eye
(the left one, of course, for his right has a patch)
notes hole and position,
as down to his mission
he swoops like a hawk, the bold fizzer to catch.

Whamsplatch! It's a bull's-eye!
"Well stopped!" hear the crowd cry.
One whack from the mallet: That bung is in tight.
Ambrose Spike takes the floor,
holding high Skipper's paw.
"Our friend saved the day for the banquet tonight!"

Meanwhile in Mossflower
our abbot announces,
"Back to the Abbey, my friends.
This *Bobbatan Quest*
is halfway done;
at Redwall, the *Weary Nod* ends!"

Bewildered but obedient,
they retrace their way
on the path they traveled earlier that day!
Relieved, but very puzzled,
Foremole gives a groan:
"Questan, Bobban an' Nodden, far away from 'ome!"

Matthias silently agrees:
They've been led, but where?
Trudging around in woodland for a thing that isn't there!
When a mouse grows older,
his memory often slips.
But never would the abbot hear that from Matthias' lips.

Loyalty and affection
for their aged friend,
trusting him far beyond any journey's end.
Faithful and unfailing,
hoping to be home soon,
they wend along together through acres of afternoon.

Now for the abbot's cake —
Will wonders never cease?
Friar Hugo, his ladle waves: "'Twill be my masterpiece!"
Twenty mice sift the flour,
mix it for over an hour.
"Bring me fruit, greensap milk. This cake'll be as big as a tower!"

"Get out, Bungo, you wretch,
and leave those nuts alone!"
"Get him, stop him, Basil! Too late, the villain's flown."
The hare is very busy
rolling soft marchpane.
Secretly, Bungo the brigand comes sneaking back again.

Seashells and icing rosebuds
fashioned with loving pride,
green, pink and yellow, 'round the cake's broadside.
Blending beech and hazelnuts
with mounds of honeycream,
"Bungo's on the loose again!" hear Hugo's panicked scream.

Bungo the bandit is everywhere,
plundering without a care,
an outlaw with two sticky paws and tiny ruthless jaws.
Dodging 'round the ovens,
or hiding 'neath a table,
nothing edible is safe from one so small and able.

Friar Hugo and Basil Hare
are working as a team,
finishing the icing, smoothing off the cream.
They add the final rosebud,
and stand back, satisfied.
"Perfection!" squeaks fat Hugo, his face aglow with pride.

A sudden naughty chuckle
brings cries of loud dismay.
"Where's that rascal Bungo?" do I hear somebeast say.
"He must be apprehended!
Stopped at any price!"
That cake may be the abbot's, but Bungo wants first slice!

"There he goes, the villain,
behind that trolley. There!"
Like an infant moleplague bound to get his share.
Hugo swings a dishcloth,
Basil wields a broom;
between them they chase Bungo all around the room.

It's Skipper to the rescue!
Slamming the kitchen doors,
he grabs an empty icing pan firmly in both paws.
Bungo tries to scuttle by,
as swiftly as he can.
Skipper traps the molebabe neatly, underneath the pan.

"Haha!" laughs Basil,
"Hoho!" Skipper roars.
"Escape from that, if you can!"
But there's no reply,
and d'you know why?
Bungo's scraping the pan!

Meanwhile in the bell tower
Skipper's otter troop
is brewing up a caldron of extra hotroot soup.
Only an otter can make it,
it's a very old recipe,
and only an otter would taste it (rather him than me).

"Pile in pondshrimp,
leeks and onions,
wild garlic, and horseradish too!
Reed mace, starwort,
mare's tail, burr reed.
More garlic, it's good for you!"

Skipper rolls up
to take a quick sup.
"There's somethin' amiss here, mates.
Hotroot pepper, *haharr*,
that's the stuff.
It'll melt the pattern off plates!"

An otter named Riverjack,
toting a burlap sack,
has a peg on his nose and a ladle.
Hear the otter crew whoop:
"Give us good hotroot soup!"
(They've been reared on the stuff from the cradle.)

Skipper throws aside caution
as he heaps in each portion:
one, two, three, four, five, six, and more!
With eyes all astreaming
otters grinning and beaming
break out into song with a roar.

"Oh, nothin's 'otter
than an otter,
when he's suppin' hotroot soup!
His eyes pop out,
his ears perk up,
an' his tail curls in a loop!

"So fill me bowl
up to the top,
an' add another scoop
of pipin' hot,
that hits the spot,
I'll finish yours if you cannot,
o' good old hotroot sooooooooooooup!"

Redwall's late-noon shadows
dissolve to evening shade.
All around the Abbey final plans are made.
Neat nimble squirrels,
like fireflies in flight,
set walltorch, candle, and lantern alight.

Noisy Sam keeps vigil
atop the rampart wall,
peering at the path below, ready to give his call.
Redwall stands awaiting
and anticipating
any sign of the questors, at all.

Young ones wriggling,
squiggling, giggling,
squirm, all agog and excited.
"Tonight's the night!"
their elders laugh.
One can see, even they are delighted.

There's Bungo the bold,
clutching tight hold
of a doorpost, wailing and howling.
As Abbey babes all
are led to the tub,
he clings like a limpet there, growling.

"Ho mercy, ho spurr me,
  oi'll purrish an' drown!
Then yew woant see this molechoild no more!"
His mum and Cornflower
with cunning and power
simply tickle his paws from the door.

Protesting and pleading
with no beast aheeding,
the mucky-faced Bungo in horror
yells out, "Ho no,
go 'way, let oi go!
An' oi promise t'get barthed tormorrer!"

Whizzpop, girgle, splosh!
Straight into the wash,
Bungo's firmly tubbed up with the rest
where immediately he
is a pirate at sea,
a bath-splashing, sud-covered pest!

Flinging the soap
and blowing bubbles,
Bungo adds to bathtime troubles.
Squirting water
at all about:
"Oi loikes it in yurr, oi b'aint cummen owt!"

Pushed from the kitchens
by strong willing paws,
travel trundling trolleys and carts,
each laden with dishes
of all that's delicious,
from savory flans to sweet tarts.

"They'll be comin' soon,
   aye, an' so will the moon,"
Ambrose muses, whilst rolling a cask.
The sun sinks low
in the western sky,
   deep red from its long day's task.

They've decked Great Hall
from lintel to wall
with streamers, banners, and flowers.
But where's the abbot
and his three chums?
Missing, for hours and hours!

How far to Redwall?
Wearypawed and slow,
out of the darkened woodlands, down the path they go.
The abbot sympathizes,
"Soon we'll take a rest.
I'm sorry to cause you worry with my silly quest."

As Foremole smiles
and Constance shrugs,
Matthias raises his paw.
"See, the spire,
'tis the Abbey ahead!
What are we dawdling for?"

Revived by the sight
of Redwall that night,
four travelers step out apace,
whilst high in the skies,
like small jeweled eyes,
the stars watch down from space.

"Hoorah, they're here!"
bellows Noisy Sam
from his perch on the rampart wall.
"Open the gates!
Sound the two bells!
Come running, one and all!"

Redwallers throng
to the threshold
to welcome their friends inside.
Abbey bells ring
brazen greetings,
as the doors swing open wide.

Constance the badger,
Matthias and Foremole
troop in with a smile and a sigh,
as off to Great Hall
flock Redwallers all
with their abbot held shoulder high.

"We never found out
what the quest was about,"
says Matthias. "But at least
we kept our abbot
distracted all day,
so our friends could make his feast."

From colored lanterns,
flowers and food
and each young shining face,
to every elder,
clad in their best,
Great Hall is a magical place.

"Surprise! Surprise!"
See the abbot's eyes;
do they twinkle knowingly?
"Good gracious!" he says
as he stands back aways.
"Well, I never! Is all this for me?"

Baby Bungo appears,
scrubbed from tail to ears,
and his abbot's paw he takes.
"Oi did it all
furr yew," he fibs,
"tho' some of 'em 'elped wi' the cakes!"

'Mid laughter and cheers
from his Abbey peers,
the abbot walks to his place.
Bungo sits on his knee
whilst reverently
they recite the Redwall grace.

*"Seasons of plenty,
days of peace
in Redwall, may these never cease.
Good comradeship,
long life and health:
our Abbey's precious wealth.*

*"From winter's white
to summer's gold,
from spring to autumn, we uphold
these bounties
Mother Nature brings.
Respect her earth and living things."*

The prayer is over,
marked by when
Noisy Sam roars out, "Amen!"
And loud but clear
above the din,
Basil gives the word: "Dig in!"

Oh, was there ever
such a feast!
Each Redwaller, each Abbeybeast
raises his and her beaker
in a toast:
"To the abbot we love most!"

They're supping the soups
and serving the salads,
whilst choirs of otters sing comical ballads.
Cutting the cakes
and serving the sweets,
as magical mole does conjuring feats.

Chewing and chattering,
munching and laughing,
nibbling, sipping, gobbling, quaffing.
"Hey, try some of that!"
"Here, have more of this!"
Bungo gives Constance a big sticky kiss.

Here's strawberry fizz,
there's October ale,
and dandelion cordial, by the pail.
Hot damson pudding,
cold junket sweet,
warm blueberry scones, they're nice to eat.

There's the abbot's fine cake,
and on Bungo's advice
he allows the small charmer to take first slice.
So the banquet rolls on
into late-night hours,
'midst laughter, lanterns, singing, and flowers.

A single bell
tolls midnight's knell,
yet some old friends are able.
There's still one or two
doing justice to
what's left on the banquet table.

Basil "Stag" Hare
and Skipper are there,
Matthias, Cornflower also,
Ambrose, Foremole,
Constance too.
(It's awfully late, you know.)

Most of the young,
with the elders,
have wandered off weary to beds,
but still a number,
seated in slumber,
droop and nod their heads.

Baby Bungo's asleep
on the abbot's knee,
both of them snoring uproariously,
when from the sleeve
of the abbot's robe...
a parchment scroll slides free!

The scroll rolls on the table,
close to Cornflower's cup.
"What is it?" comes the whisper. "Go on, pick it up!
Our abbot's rule you may recall:
'There are no secrets in Redwall!'
We're sure that if you read it, he won't mind at all!"

Opening wide the parchment,
Cornflower reads each word,
not aloud, but to herself, so not a sound is heard.
"Speak up, m'dear!" calls Basil.
"State clearly what you see."
The pretty mouse is lost for words, she's laughing helplessly.

"Oh, dearie me, haha heehee!
  Oh, oh my aching jaws!"
The parchment slips onto the table from her shaking paws.
"The abb...haha...the abbot
  has heeheeheeheehee!
  Oh hohoho, hahahaha! Look for yourself and see!"

They gaze amazed,
bemused and dazed,
and can't believe their eyes!
They thought their abbot
was old and silly.
Now they know he is ancient and wise.

Jumble me up and turn me about,
if you wish to find the key.
A solution to the quest comes out,
move the letters and you will see.

BOBBATAN QUEST

B	becomes	A
O	becomes	B
B	becomes	B
B	becomes	O
A	becomes	T
T	becomes	S
A	becomes	B
N	becomes	A
Q	becomes	N
U	becomes	Q
E	becomes	U
S	becomes	E
T	becomes	T

ABBOT'S BANQUET

WEARY NOD

The letter W is where the R should be
and where the R was, place the D;
put W where the D used to go.
So now, my friends, you know!

WEARY NOD
READY NOW

Put the words together,
the answer's clear somehow.
It fits together perfectly!
Abbot's Banquet, Ready Now!

So there you have it.
I remember that feast.
Wasn't our abbot a clever old beast
to make up his riddle
and go on the quest?
Sometimes it's not just the young who know best.

Good-bye, my friends,
come back sometime.
Maybe I'll read you another rhyme.
Our names and address,
should you wish to call:
Bungo and Sam, the Abbey. Redwall.